W9-BRU-611

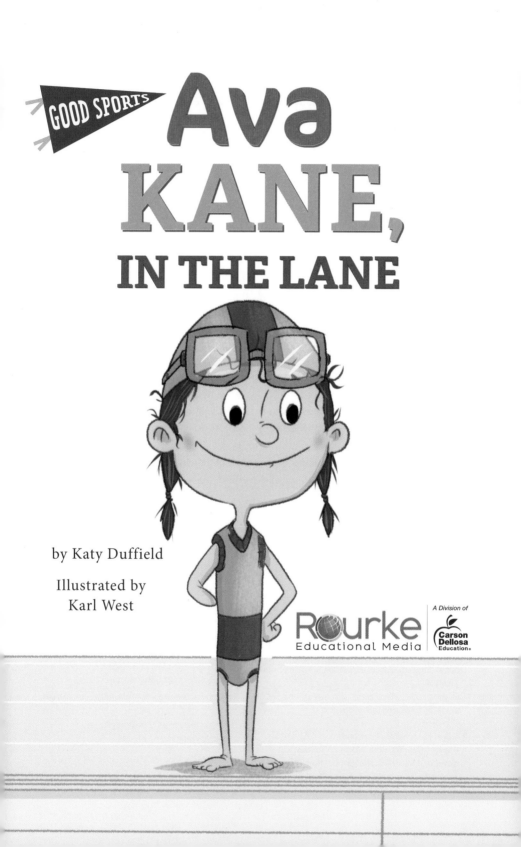

GOOD SPORTS

Ava KANE,
IN THE LANE

by Katy Duffield

Illustrated by
Karl West

Rourke
Educational Media

A Division of
Carson
Dellosa
Education

Dear Guardian/Educator,
Introduce your child to the wonderful world of reading with our leveled readers. Your growing reader will be continuously engaged as he or she is guided from one level to the next. Each level is carefully built to provide your child with the reading skills and knowledge to be a confident reader! Ultimately, we want your child to develop a love of reading.

Level 1 *Learning to Read*
High frequency words, basic sentences, large type, labels, full color illustrations to help young readers better comprehend the text

Level 2 *Beginning to Read Alone*
Short sentences, familiar words, simple plot, easy-to-read fonts

Level 3 *Reading on Your Own*
Short paragraphs, easy-to-follow plots, vocabulary is increasingly challenging, exciting stories

Level 4 *Proficient Reader*
Chapters, engaging stories, challenging vocabulary, multiple text features

Reading should be a pleasurable experience. A child who enjoys reading reads more, and a child who reads more becomes a better reader. Your child will grow with exposure to broad vocabulary and literary techniques, and will develop deeper critical thinking and comprehension skills. We are excited to be a part of your child's reading journey.

Happy reading,
Rourke Educational Media

© 2021 Rourke Educational Media

All rights reserved. No part of this book may be reproduced or utilized in any form or by any means, electronic or mechanical including photocopying, recording, or by any information storage and retrieval system without permission in writing from the publisher.

www.rourkeeducationalmedia.com

Edited by: Madison Capitano
Interior layout by: Rhea Magaro-Wallace
Cover and interior illustrations by: Karl West

Library of Congress PCN Data

Ava Kane, In the Lane / Katy Duffield
(Good Sports)
ISBN 978-1-73163-810-6 (hard cover)(alk. paper)
ISBN 978-1-73163-887-8 (soft cover)
ISBN 978-1-73163-964-6 (e-Book)
ISBN 978-1-73164-041-3 (ePub)
Library of Congress Control Number: 2020930051

Printed in the United States of America
01-1662011937

Table of Contents

Blobfish
Swim Team

Chapter One
Let's Swim!

My name is Ava Kane. People say I swim like a fish. Maybe that is why I am on the Blobfish swim team. We have practice today. I can't wait!

Coach Goats blows his whistle.

"Let's swim!" he calls.

I jump into the pool.

SPLASH!

But my teammate, Alonso, doesn't.

Alonso holds onto the **ladder**. He carefully tiptoes down the steps. He clings tightly to the pool wall.

I swim over to Alonso.

"Are you okay?" I ask.

Alonso nods.

But he doesn't look okay.

He looks scared.

Chapter Two

Let's Get Squishy!

"You can share my swim **lane**," I say.

But Alonso keeps holding the wall.

I want to help him. But I don't know how.

Then, I see a squishy rubber fish by the side of the pool. It's Blobbie! He's the Blobfish team's own blobfish. Now I know what to do!

I swim to Blobbie. I put my **goggles** on him. I lift up the fish and jiggle him in the air.

"Look, Alonso!" I call.

Alonso smiles.

Blobbie gives me another idea.

I puff out my cheeks. I flap my arms. I bounce in the water.

"Do I look like a blobfish?" I ask.

Alonso giggles. He makes a blobfish face too. Then, he lets go of the wall! He even bounces in the water.

Chapter Three
Blobbie for the Win!

"Watch this!" I tell Alonso.

I put my head under the water. I make my blobfish face.

Alonso tries it too!

Then, Alonso takes a
big breath. He puffs out
his cheeks. He moves his
arms and kicks his feet. He
swims to the wall and back.

"Way to go, Alonso!" I yell.
Once Alonso is in the
water, he is a great swim
partner.

He gets my **kickboard**

for me.

Sometimes, he swims

faster. Sometimes, I do.

I love to swim.

But it's always more fun

with Alonso on my team!

Bonus Stuff!

Glossary

Can you find these pictures in the story?

Can you find these words in the story?

goggles

kickboard

ladder

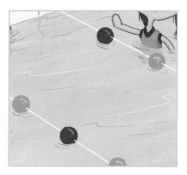

lane

Activity: Fishy Fun

Make a fun paper fish!

Supplies

- construction paper
- scissors
- decorating supplies: crayons, markers, glitter, sequins

Directions

1. Cut construction paper into a square.
2. Fold the square diagonally. Unfold. Fold diagonally in the other direction. Unfold.
3. Fold in half. Unfold.
4. Push sides in to create a triangle.
5. Take the bottom right corner of the triangle and fold it toward the center.
6. Repeat with the bottom left corner. Flip it over.
7. Now, decorate your fish!

Discussion Questions

1. Why did Ava put her swim goggles on Blobbie? How did that help Alonso?

2. What other ways did Ava help Alonso relax in the pool?

3. Have you ever been afraid of something? Did someone help you feel better? What did they do to help you?

About the Author

Katy Duffield has written more than thirty books for kids. She wishes she could swim like a blobfish! Katy lives with her family in Arkansas.

About the Illustrator

Karl West is an illustrator based in Weymouth, England. He lives with his fiancé and their Chihuahua, Chewi, just a stone's throw from the sea.